How will George compete in the bike race without a bike?

"Bess, where were you?" George demanded.

Bess stopped in her tracks. "What's the matter? I was talking to Brenda out front. She said she had to interview me about the race. All she did was ask me a bunch of dumb questions, though."

"Where is George's bike?" Nancy asked her.

Bess frowned. "What do you mean? It's right here—" She gasped. "Oh, no! Where did it go?"

"I was right!" George said miserably. "Someone stole it!"

The Nancy Drew Notebooks

Available from Simon & Schuster

THE
NANCY DREW
NOTEBOOKS®

#59

The Bike Race Mystery

CAROLYN KEENE
ILLUSTRATED BY PAUL CASALE

Aladdin Paperbacks
New York   London   Toronto   Sydney

First Aladdin Paperbacks edition April 2004
Copyright © 2004 by Simon & Schuster, Inc

ALADDIN PAPERBACKS
An imprint of Simon & Schuster
Children's Publishing Division
1230 Avenue of the Americas
New York, NY 10020

The text of this book was set in Excelsior.

Printed in the United States of America
10 9 8 7 6 5 4 3 2 1

Library of Congress Control Number 2003113816

ISBN 0-689-86343-8

1

Bike Mania

Eight-year-old Nancy Drew strapped on her bike helmet. It was light blue with stickers all over it. "I'm ready to go," she announced.

Her best friends, Bess Marvin and George Fayne, put on their bike helmets too. So did Hannah Gruen, the Drews' housekeeper.

"I hope I still remember how to ride this thing." Hannah patted the handlebars of her silver ten-speed bike. "I hardly take it out anymore."

"I've been practicing on my bike every single day," Bess said.

"Me, too," George piped up.

"Me, three," Nancy added. "The big bike race is this Saturday."

It was spring break. At the end of the break week, Nancy and her friends planned to compete in a bike race and bike rodeo. The bike rodeo was an obstacle course that kids had to go through on their bikes. Both the race and rodeo were being held by a bike shop called Bike Mania.

The girls and Hannah were all on their way to Bike Mania now. Today was the last day to sign up for the race and rodeo.

"Wouldn't it be so cool if one of us won the grand prize?" George said as she straddled her bike.

"What's the grand prize? A million dollars?" Bess said eagerly.

George cracked up. "No, silly. It's a brand-new mountain bike."

"I wonder what color the mountain bike will be?" Nancy said. She hoped it would be blue. Blue was her favorite color.

"We'll find out soon. Come on, girls, let's hit the road!" Hannah said.

"Come on, Pink Rocket!" Bess exclaimed.

"Pink Rocket? Who's Pink Rocket?" Nancy asked her, puzzled.

"That's what she named her bike," George explained.

Nancy giggled.

Hannah pedaled down the Drews' driveway. The three girls got on their bikes and followed close behind.

It was a beautiful spring day. The sun was shining brightly, and there were fluffy white clouds in the air. The yards in Nancy's neighborhood were filled with daffodils, tulips, and other pretty flowers.

Bike Mania was on a quiet street halfway between Nancy's house and downtown River Heights. When Hannah and the girls arrived at the shop, they pedaled through the parking lot that was behind the store. They parked their bikes at the bike rack.

There wasn't enough space at the rack for George's bike, though. So George offered to park her bike in the grass. "It'll be okay here," she said to the others.

Inside the store, customers were checking out rows and rows of shiny new bikes. Nancy went right to the kids' section. She loved her own bike, which she had gotten for her birthday. But Bike Mania had some really high-tech kids' bikes. They looked supercool.

"Check out the frame on this one," George said, pointing to one of the bikes. "And check out the wheels on *that* one!"

"I think the color of a bicycle is the most important thing," Bess said. "I wish I could have a different color bike for every day of the week!"

Nancy giggled. Bess and George were so different that sometimes Nancy couldn't believe they were cousins.

"Can I help you girls?"

Nancy glanced up. A man was standing behind the counter. He had curly dark-blond hair that came down to his chin and a thin mustache. He was dressed in a tight red bicycle jersey and matching shorts.

"Welcome to Bike Mania!" the man said. "I'm Jesse Hamilton. Are you girls looking for a new bike?"

"Yes! I mean, no," George replied. "I want to *win* a new bike. In the race, that is."

Mr. Hamilton smiled. "You must be here

to sign up for the bike race and rodeo. Step right up, ladies."

Nancy and her friends walked up to the counter. Mr. Hamilton handed each of them an entry form and a pen.

"I'll need your name, age, school, home address, phone number, your mom or dad's name, and an adult's signature," Mr. Hamilton explained. He winked at Hannah. "I guess that would be yours."

Hannah laughed. "Yes."

"And I'll need a five-dollar entry fee from each of you girls," Mr. Hamilton went on. "You'll be happy to know it's for a good cause. All the money I collect from this race will go toward the Re-Cycles program."

Hannah reached into her purse and pulled out three five-dollar bills. She handed them to Mr. Hamilton. "What exactly is the Re-Cycles program?" she asked him.

Mr. Hamilton pointed to a poster on the wall. It had a photo of a blond girl standing next to a red bike. She was wearing bike shorts, a matching jersey, and sunglasses. She was carrying a bike helmet in her arms. Under the photo, a caption said: SPREAD THE JOY OF CYCLING BY RE-CYCLING! There was a Web site address under it.

"Re-Cycles is a program I run out of this shop," Mr. Hamilton replied. "We fix up used bicycles so they're as good as new. Then we donate them to kids in River Heights who can't afford to buy bikes of their own."

"What a great idea!" Hannah exclaimed.

Mr. Hamilton grinned. "Thanks! Since we started the program, we've given away almost fifty bikes. You should check out our Web site. It has a lot of information about our program."

"Do you fix up the old bikes all by yourself?" Nancy asked him curiously.

Mr. Hamilton shook his head. "Nope. Come this way. I'll introduce you to my special helpers."

The girls followed him through a blue door. There was a sign on it with big, hand-painted letters that said PRIVATE!

They found themselves in a huge room filled with bikes. Some of the bikes were rusty and dented. Others had flat tires.

Every single bike had *something* wrong with it, Nancy noted.

Then she noticed two kids in the back corner of the room. One of them was a skinny boy with big shoulders and sun-bleached blond hair. Nancy guessed he was twelve or thirteen. The other kid was a girl about Nancy's age. She had honey-blond hair pulled back with a pink scrunchie and barrettes.

The boy and the girl were working on the old bikes. They were both wearing white T-shirts and jeans covered with black grease. There were tools all around them on the floor.

"This is my daughter, Tia," Mr. Hamilton said, pointing to the girl. "And that's my son, Slam."

"Slam?" George murmured. "What a cool name!"

"He's really Stephen, but he doesn't like to be called that anymore," Mr. Hamilton explained in a low voice.

Tia gave Nancy and the others a shy smile. Slam barely looked up from the bike he was working on.

"Tia and Slam help me fix up all the bikes for the Re-Cycles program," Mr. Hamilton added.

"That is so awesome!" Nancy said eagerly. "I wish I knew how to fix bikes."

"I'll be happy to teach you, anytime," Mr. Hamilton told her.

After saying good-bye to Slam and Tia, Nancy and the others returned to the main part of the store. They finished filling out their forms for the race and rodeo.

"I can't wait till Saturday," George said to Nancy and Bess. "I really, really hope I win!"

"There's no way you're going to win, Fayne!"

Nancy spun around at the sound of the strange voice. A boy with short black hair was standing nearby. He was wearing silver bike shorts and a black sweatshirt. He had a smirk on his face.

"Oh, it's you, Lucas," George mumbled. She didn't sound very happy.

"Do you know this boy?" Hannah asked George.

George sighed. "Everyone, this is Lucas Wylie. His family just moved across the street from us. He goes to the Winslow School for Boys. Lucas, this is Nancy, Bess, and Ms. Gruen."

"Hi," Lucas said. "Like I was saying, Fayne. There's no way you're going to win. Because *I'm* going to win."

George put her hands on her hips and glared at him. "Oh, yeah?"

Lucas grinned. "Yeah!"

"You want to make a bet?" George asked him. "The winner has to buy the loser whatever they want at the Double Dip!" The Double Dip was the yummiest ice cream parlor in River Heights.

Lucas nodded. "You're on! You'd better start saving your money right now, Fayne. Because I'm going to order the biggest hot fudge sundae on the menu!"

Lucas cracked up and walked away. Nancy watched as he strapped on his bike helmet and left the store.

"What a jerk!" she said to George.

"What a superjerk!" Bess agreed.

George shrugged. "I don't care, as long as I beat him in the race. And I will!"

"Okay, girls, why don't we forget about

Lucas?" Hannah broke in. "Let's give the forms to Mr. Hamilton and get going. Your parents are expecting you home."

"Okay, Hannah," the girls chimed together.

They handed the forms to Mr. Hamilton and said good-bye. Then they headed out of the store, chatting excitedly about the race.

"I'm going to practice twice as hard for the rest of the week!" Nancy told her friends.

"Me, too," George added. "Plus, I'm going to—"

She stopped suddenly. "Oh, no!"

"Oh no, *what*?" Bess demanded.

"My bike! It's gone!" George cried.

2

Missing!

Nancy stared at the spot on the grass where George had left her bike. George was right. It was gone!

Just then, Nancy saw something out of the corner of her eye. Across the parking lot, there was a red-haired girl riding away on a white bike. The bike looked just like George's!

George noticed the red-haired girl too. "That's my bike!" she shouted.

Nancy started chasing after the girl on the bike. "Hey! You on the white bike! Stop right there!" she yelled.

The red-haired girl screeched to a halt

and turned around. Nancy, Bess, George, and Hannah caught up to her.

The girl looked at them and blinked. "Hi. What's the matter?" she said in a high, breathless voice.

"You stole George's bike!" Bess accused her.

George nodded. "Yeah! That's my bike!"

The girl blinked again. "*Your* bike? Oh! I thought it was one of the bikes for sale. I was taking it for a test drive!" she explained.

Hannah frowned. "Why did you think it was for sale?"

The girl shrugged. "I don't know. It wasn't parked at the bike rack. And it wasn't locked up or anything." She giggled nervously.

"There wasn't room for my bike on the rack, and anyway, I forgot my bike lock at home," George said. "We were just going into the store for a minute."

"Oh," the girl said.

"So I guess I'll take my bike back now," George added.

The girl giggled again. "Sure. Sorry!"

She swung her leg over the bike and got off. She paused for a moment before handing the bike over to George.

"Where'd you get it, anyway?" the girl asked George. "This bike, I mean. They don't make this model anymore."

"It used to belong to my cousin," George explained. "He gave it to me when he got a new bike."

"I've been begging my mom and dad for this exact same model." The girl sighed. "I saw it once in a magazine, and I really love it!" She blinked at George. "You wouldn't consider selling it, would you?"

George shook her head. "No way! I really love it too. Besides, it's my good luck bike. I won a race on it last summer. And I'm going to win the Bike Mania race on it this Saturday!"

The girl hung her head. "Oh, well. If you ever change your mind, my name's Marianne Blair."

With that, Marianne waved good-bye and took off down the street.

George turned to Nancy. "*That* was weird."

"Yeah," Nancy agreed. "But at least you got your bike back!"

"This'll just take a minute, I promise," George said. "Then we can head over to the Double Dip for ice cream!"

It was Tuesday morning. George, Bess, and Nancy had gotten permission to ride over to Bike Mania by themselves.

George couldn't find her bike lock anywhere at home. She and her parents had searched all over the garage. But the bike lock was nowhere to be found.

So Mr. and Mrs. Fayne had given George some money to buy a new bike lock. George had asked Nancy and Bess to come with her.

At Bike Mania, the bike rack was all filled up again. So the three girls parked their bikes in the grass.

"I'll stay out here and guard them, just in case someone else tries to ride them," Bess offered.

"Good idea," Nancy agreed.

Nancy and George took their helmets off and headed into the store. Inside, the room

16

was packed with customers. Slam was behind the counter, leafing through a magazine. He was wearing a red T-shirt that said BE A BIKE MANIAC!

Slam glanced up. "Hey," he said in a bored-sounding voice.

"Is your dad around?" Nancy asked him.

Slam shook his head. "He's out doing some stuff. Can I help you?"

"I need a new bike lock," George explained. "Can you show me what you have?"

"Sure," Slam replied.

Slam reached into a case and took out a few bike locks. He began explaining the different kinds to George.

Just then, Nancy felt someone tap her on the shoulder. "Ahem! I'd like to ask you a few questions," said a familiar-sounding voice.

Nancy turned around. It was Brenda Carlton.

Brenda was in Nancy, Bess, and George's third-grade class at Carl Sandburg Elementary School. Brenda's father was the publisher of the River Heights newspaper.

Nancy always tried to be nice and friendly to Brenda. But Brenda was hardly ever nice and friendly back. In fact, she was usually pretty snooty and mean.

Nancy noticed that Brenda was holding a small notebook and a pen. "Hi to you, too, Brenda," Nancy said. "What kind of questions do you want to ask me?"

Brenda tossed her long, dark hair over her shoulders. "I'm working for my father this week," she replied. "I'm writing a very, *very* important article about the bike race."

"Oh!" Nancy said, surprised.

"I'm interviewing all the people in the race," Brenda added. "You and George and Bess are in it, right? Can I interview you guys?"

George was still checking out bike locks. She glanced over her shoulder at Brenda. "Sure," she said. "What do you want to ask us?"

"Fire away!" Nancy said to Brenda.

Brenda poised her pen over her pad. "So, Nancy. Are you excited about being in the race?" she asked.

Nancy smiled. "Definitely!"

Brenda nodded. "Uh-huh. Are you still going to be friends with George if she beats you?"

Nancy's smile turned into a big frown. "Of course! What kind of question is *that*?"

Brenda pointed her pen at George. "So, George. Your turn. Have you ever cheated in a race?"

"*What?*" George gasped.

"How far would you go to win *this* race?" Brenda went on. "Would you cheat? Lie? Mess up someone else's bike?"

George put her hands on her hips. "Brenda Carlton! What kind of interview *is* this?"

"It's my job to ask the tough questions, people," Brenda explained. She turned her pad to a clean page. "Okay, now, where's Bess?"

"Outside," Nancy replied. "But if you ask her more questions like these, she's not going to answer you, either!"

Brenda smiled slyly. "We'll see." She gave the girls a little wave and headed outside.

Nancy shook her head. "Can't she be nice, for once?" she asked George.

"No way. She's Brenda Carlton!" George replied.

George turned her attention back to the bike locks lying on the counter. She finally decided on one and paid Slam for it.

"Thank you!" George said to him.

"Sure," Slam mumbled. He barely looked up from the magazine he was reading.

Nancy and George went outside to where Bess was guarding their bikes.

Nancy's bike was lying in the grass. So was Bess's bike.

But Bess was nowhere to be seen. And neither was George's bike!

3

A Pink Clue

Oh, no! Not again!" George cried.

"Where's Bess?" Nancy asked, glancing around.

"She was supposed to be guarding our bikes!" George moaned. "My bike is gone! It's been stolen—again!"

"Maybe Bess just took your bike for a ride," Nancy said hopefully.

Just then, Nancy spotted Bess coming down the driveway toward the parking lot. She was not riding George's bike.

"Hey!" Bess said, waving.

"Bess, where were you?" George demanded.

Bess stopped in her tracks. "What's the matter? I was talking to Brenda out front. She said she had to interview me about the race. All she did was ask me a bunch of dumb questions, though."

"Where is George's bike?" Nancy asked her.

Bess frowned. "What do you mean? It's right here—" She gasped. "Oh, no! Where did it go?"

"I was right!" George said miserably. "Someone stole it!"

"Oh my gosh, I'm so sorry," Bess apologized. "Brenda and I just started walking and talking. I didn't mean to leave the bikes for so long. I'm so sorry, George!" She looked as though she was about to cry.

Nancy grabbed George's arm. "Bess, you stay here with the bikes. Don't move! George, come on. Maybe the thief is still around here somewhere."

Nancy and George took off running. They searched the entire parking lot. Then they went out in front of the store and looked up and down the street. George's bike was nowhere to be seen.

Then they went inside the store. Slam was still behind the counter, reading his magazine.

"Slam!" Nancy said breathlessly. "Have you seen George's bike?"

"It's a white ABT Road Lizard," George explained quickly.

Slam looked impressed. "ABT Road Lizard? Wow, you have one of those? They don't make them anymore," he said.

"I know, I know! My Road Lizard is missing, though. It was parked out back. Now it's gone!" George exclaimed.

"That's a bummer," Slam said. "Sorry! I'll let my dad know when he gets back. I guess you could have used that bike lock sooner, huh?"

"Thanks, Slam. Come on, George," Nancy said. She and George headed back outside.

They found Bess standing guard over her pink bike and Nancy's blue bike. "Did you find George's bike?" Bess asked immediately.

Nancy shook her head. "No."

"It's all my fault," Bess moaned. "I am so dumb!"

"You're not dumb, Bess. You just made a mistake," George told her.

Then Nancy got an idea. She knelt down and ran her hand over the grass. She found the spot where George's bike had been parked.

It had rained last night, so the ground was still wet and soft. George's bike tires had left two dents in the ground.

Nancy looked closer. There was something shiny lying in the dent the back tire had made.

Nancy picked it up. It was a pink barrette with a zigzag design.

"It's a clue!" Nancy exclaimed. "Whoever stole your bike dropped this barrette, George!"

"How do you know it wasn't there before?" Bess asked her.

"Because it was lying in the dent of George's bike. And because it's superclean. If it had been there before, it would be all dirty and muddy from the rain last night," Nancy replied.

"Nancy, you are so smart!" Bess said.

George frowned. "I bet I know who did it.

That girl from yesterday who was riding my bike. Marianne something."

"Marianne Blair?" Nancy said. "We don't have any proof against her, George. We can't just accuse her of being the thief. We have to talk to her, first."

"Yeah, but she said she wanted my bike. My superfast white ABT Road Lizard bike. She *has* to be the thief," George insisted.

Just then, Nancy had a feeling that someone was listening to their conversation.

She whirled around. Brenda Carlton was standing behind a big oak tree. She had her notebook in hand, and she was scribbling like mad.

"Brenda!" Nancy cried out.

Brenda kept scribbling. "Keep talking. This is going to be a great story for the newspaper. 'Mysterious Bike Thief Hits River Heights!'"

"Quit being nosy!" Bess exclaimed. "We're trying to find George's bike."

"Yeah, Brenda. It's rude to listen to other people's conversations," Nancy pointed out.

"I know how you guys can find Marianne Blair," Brenda said suddenly.

Nancy gasped. "You do?" she said, surprised.

Brenda tossed her hair over her shoulders. "Her mom and my mom are friends. I can tell you where she lives," she offered.

"Really?" George said hopefully.

Brenda nodded. "On one condition. You take me with you. I want to get the behind-the-scenes scoop on this story! 'Eight-Year-Old Detective Nabs Eight-Year-Old Bike Thief.'"

Nancy was the best detective at Carl Sandburg Elementary School. She had solved lots of mysteries before. George and Bess always helped her. The three of them were a great detective team.

Nancy had never solved a mystery with Brenda before, though. In fact, Brenda was often one of her suspects.

Nancy, George, and Bess exchanged a glance. Nancy knew that her friends were thinking the same thing she was. Could they trust Brenda? And more important, did they want Brenda tagging along and writing about them?

George shrugged. Bess shrugged too.

Nancy knew the final decision was up to her.

"Okay," Nancy said finally. "I guess you can come along, Brenda. But you have to promise us one thing. Let us do all the detective work. You have to stay out of the way."

"Sure, I'll stay out of the way," Brenda promised. "No problem!" She tucked her notebook and pen into her pocket. "Come on, let's go to Marianne's house. We have a mystery to solve!"

Nancy, George, and Bess exchanged another glance. Nancy hoped she wasn't making a big mistake by bringing Brenda along!

"This is it!" Brenda whispered.

Brenda, Nancy, and Bess had walked their bikes to 43 Lee Avenue. It was a pink house just down the block from Bike Mania. George had walked along with them.

Nancy stopped and popped her bike's kickstand. "This is where Marianne Blair lives? Are you sure?" she asked Brenda in a low voice.

Brenda nodded. "Yes, I'm sure. You guys stay here; I'll check things out!"

"Brenda, you promised to stay out of the way," Nancy reminded her.

But before Nancy could stop her, Brenda had gotten off her bike and run down the Blairs' driveway. She disappeared into their backyard.

"She's trespassing," Bess pointed out.

"Plus she's not letting *us* be the detectives," George added.

Nancy sighed. "Oh, well. Let's just knock on the door and see if Marianne's home. We can ask her some questions."

Nancy and Bess locked their bikes to an iron fence. Then they and George walked through the yard toward the front door.

Just then, Brenda came running from behind the house. "Guess what!" she said excitedly. "I've solved the mystery!"

4

In Search of the Thief

Nancy stared at Brenda. "What do you mean you solved the mystery?" she demanded.

"I mean, I've found George's bike," Brenda replied. "Aren't you glad you guys brought me along?"

"Where is it? Where's my bike?" George asked her excitedly.

Brenda grinned. "Follow me!"

Nancy, Bess, and George followed Brenda down the driveway. Nancy didn't like going on the Blairs' property without their permission. But if George's bike really was back there, she thought she should check it out.

Brenda stopped in front of the garage. The garage door was open.

"See?" Brenda said triumphantly. She pointed into the shadowy darkness of the garage.

Nancy peered inside. She saw piles of old, dusty boxes. She saw a rack of skis and poles. She saw an old baby stroller. She saw some gardening tools.

Then, in the corner, she saw a white bike.

"Brenda!" Nancy said after a moment. "That's not a kid's bike. That's a grown-up bike!"

"What? No way," Brenda said.

George nodded. "Nancy's right. That's a grown-up bike. Mine is a lot smaller."

"Oh." Brenda frowned. "*Well*. Anyone could have made that mistake. It's super-dark in there."

"I guess we'll keep looking," Bess said, shrugging. "Let's get out of here. We were just about to see if Marianne was home."

The four girls ran quickly around to the front yard. Nancy knocked on the door.

No one answered. Nancy knocked again. Still, no one answered.

"No one's home," Nancy sighed.

Brenda was scribbling something in her notebook. She began reading it out loud. "'The Mystery Dream Team pursued their main suspect to her house at Forty-three Lee Avenue. They thought they found the missing bicycle in her garage. But it turned out to be a false lead.'" She glanced up with a grin. "Isn't this brilliant? I just came up with it."

"I wonder where Marianne is?" George said, ignoring Brenda. "Maybe she's taking a long bike ride. On *my* bike!"

"I know another place we could try," Brenda said. "The Double Dip. Marianne loves the Pink Bubble Gum Sundaes there."

"How do you know that?" Bess asked her.

"Because I know everything," Brenda replied with a grin. "And because our moms took us there once, and Marianne ordered two of them."

After lunch Nancy, Bess, George, and Brenda got permission from their parents to go to the Double Dip. When they got there, the

Double Dip was packed with kids. But Marianne Blair was nowhere in sight.

"Hmm, another false lead," Brenda said. She scribbled something into her notebook. "We're closing in on Marianne, though. I feel it in my bones!"

There was a waitress wiping down the counter. Nancy walked up to her. "Excuse me. Have you seen a girl in here with long, curly red hair?" she asked.

The waitress frowned. "Hmm, let me think. Blue eyes? Lots of freckles? A little shorter than you?"

Nancy nodded eagerly. "Yes!"

"She was here about an hour ago," the waitress said. "Ordered two Pink Bubble Gum Sundaes. She left her backpack here, so I had to go out into the parking lot and chase her down."

"Really?" Nancy thought for a moment. "Do you know if she was walking or riding a bike?"

"Oh, definitely riding a bike," the waitress replied. "I caught up to her just as she was riding away."

George came up to Nancy and the waitress.

"Was it a white bike with fat tires?" she piped up.

The waitress shrugged. "Um, I *think* it was white. But I'm not a hundred percent sure."

Nancy and George thanked the waitress. "See?" George said to Nancy. "Marianne *is* our thief."

"Maybe, maybe not," Nancy said. "Maybe Marianne already has a white bike."

Bess and Brenda joined George and Nancy. "What's going on?" Brenda asked.

Nancy twirled a lock of her blond hair. "Marianne was here, but now she's gone," she explained.

Bess sighed. "That's too bad. I think we should all get some ice cream, to cheer ourselves up."

"I agree." George sighed. "All this detective work is making me hungry!"

The four girls sat down in a booth. After looking at the menus, they all ordered sundaes. Nancy ordered a Strawberry Surprise Sundae. Bess ordered a Chocolate Lover's Sundae. George ordered a Butterscotch Burst Sundae. Brenda ordered a Very Blueberry Sundae.

"Okay, it's time to do some serious brain-storming," Nancy said when their sundaes arrived. "The bike race is Saturday. That's only four days away."

"We *have* to find my bike by then," George said. "It's my good-luck bike. Besides, even if my mom and dad bought me a *new* bike to replace it, there's no way I could get used to it by Saturday!"

"The problem is, we only have one sus-pect," Bess mused. She took a big bite of her sundae. "What if she's not the thief? We haven't even *thought* of anyone else."

Just then, there was a loud peal of laugh-ter from another booth. "Now I'm definitely going to beat George Fayne!" said a famil-iar-sounding voice.

5

Detectives in Pajamas

Nancy frowned. She knew that voice from somewhere. Who could be bragging about beating George in the race?

"Did you hear that?" George whispered. She looked over her shoulder. "Who was that? Who's talking about me?"

"This is getting juicy," Brenda said eagerly. She pulled out her reporter's notebook and started scribbling on a fresh page.

Nancy stood up and glanced around the Double Dip. She quickly found who she was looking for.

Two boys were sitting in a booth across the aisle. Nancy didn't recognize the closest boy. But she *did* recognize the other boy. It was Lucas Wylie, George's neighbor.

Nancy remembered Lucas from yesterday, when they ran into him at Bike Mania. Lucas and George had made a bet about who was going to win the bike race.

What had Lucas meant by saying, "Now I'm definitely going to beat George Fayne?" Nancy wondered.

And then an idea came to her. What if Lucas stole George's bike so he could win the race?

"You guys stay here," Nancy told George, Bess, and Brenda quietly. Then she walked up to Lucas's booth.

"Hi, Lucas," Nancy said with a friendly smile. "Remember me?"

Lucas had a big, messy chocolate mustache over his upper lip. Nancy thought it made him look really silly. She tried not to giggle.

Lucas narrowed his eyes at Nancy. "Huh? Oh, yeah, you. You're Fayne's friend. Is she chickening out on our bet?" He and his friend cracked up.

Nancy shook her head. "No, the bet's still

on. In fact, she just got her bike tuned up at Bike Mania, so it's going to run better than ever!" she fibbed.

Nancy waited to see how Lucas would react to the fib. If Lucas was the bike thief, he would know that Nancy wasn't telling the truth. He would know that George didn't just get her bike tuned up at Bike Mania, because he would have it!

But Lucas didn't act surprised at all. "Big deal," he said nastily. "Fayne's bike is a super-old model. There's no way she's going to beat me riding that piece of junk."

Lucas and his friend cracked up again. Nancy frowned. Lucas didn't seem to realize that George's bike was missing—which meant that he was innocent. But could he be putting on an act? Should Nancy add him to the suspect list anyway?

"Hey, your stuffed animals are taking over my sleeping bag!" George complained to Bess.

Bess giggled. "Sorry! I'll move them over."

"You can move some of them to my bed," Nancy suggested.

It was Tuesday night. Nancy had gotten permission for George and Bess to come over for a sleepover at her house.

The three girls had spread their sleeping bags out on the floor of Nancy's bedroom. Hannah had brought them a big bowl of buttery popcorn and glasses of chocolate milk with curlycue straws. Nancy loved sleepovers!

Nancy got her special blue detective notebook from her desk, sat down on the floor, and turned to a clean page. Her father had given her the notebook a long time ago. She liked writing her suspects and clues in it. It helped her to organize her cases.

Nancy uncapped her favorite purple pen. The purple pen had bits of glitter in it. She wrote: "The Case of George's Missing Bicycle."

"Okay," she said after a minute. "Let's write down our suspects and clues. First, we have—"

Just then there was a knock on the door. Hannah poked her head inside. "Hi, girls," she called out. "I just wanted to let you know that your other sleepover guest is here."

"Huh?" George said. "What other sleepover guest?"

The door opened wider. Brenda pranced in. She was wearing white-and-red-checked pajamas and white bunny slippers. She was carrying a sleeping bag, a backpack, and a golden-brown teddy bear.

"Hi, everyone!" Brenda said cheerfully. "Where should I put my sleeping bag? Oh, by the way, this is Esmeralda." She set her teddy bear down on the floor.

Nancy, Bess, and George all stared at Brenda. They were totally stunned. No one had invited her! How did she even know they were having a sleepover?

"Uh, hi, Brenda," Nancy said after a moment. "What, um, are you doing here?"

"After we left the Double Dip, I heard you guys whispering about having a sleepover," Brenda replied. "You know, to talk about the case and stuff. I couldn't miss *that*!"

Nancy, George, and Bess exchanged a glance. *What can we do?* Nancy thought.

Brenda's here. We're kind of stuck with her.

Brenda plopped down on the edge of Nancy's bed. "Pass the popcorn," she said. "So, what did I miss?"

"We were just talking about our suspects and clues," Bess told her.

George handed Brenda the popcorn bowl. "Nancy's writing them down in her detective notebook."

Brenda's eyes glittered. "A special detective notebook? How cool! Can I see it?"

"No," Nancy said. She hugged the notebook closer to her chest. "It's private."

"Whatever," Brenda said with a shrug. "Oh! I just remembered. I brought something that's going to help us solve this case!"

She reached into her backpack and pulled out a big book. It was called *How to Solve Mysteries*.

"There's all kinds of useful tips in here," Brenda added. "This way we'll catch the bicycle thief for sure!"

"Great," George said.

Brenda opened her book and studied the table of contents. Nancy turned her attention back to her notebook. She picked up her pen again and wrote:

SUSPECTS:
Marianne. She really, really wants George's bike!

"Listen to this." Brenda grabbed a handful of popcorn and stuffed it into her mouth. "'Chapter Four,'" she read from the book. It was hard to understand her because she had so much popcorn in her mouth. "'How to Get Your Suspects to Confess. Tip number one: Be really cool. Don't let them know you suspect them.'"

"Uh-huh," Nancy said. She wrote:

Lucas. He and George have a bet about the bike race. Maybe he stole her bike to make sure he would win the bet.

"'Tip number two: Tell your suspect a joke. That will get them to loosen up with you,'" Brenda continued reading aloud.

Bess hugged her stuffed bunny to her chest and peered over Nancy's shoulder. "What about clues? Do we have any of those?"

Nancy nodded. "Yes! We have one really good clue," she replied.

She wrote:

CLUES:
A pink barrette with a zigzag shape.

Nancy glanced up from her notebook. "We have two suspects and one clue," she announced. "Marianne, Lucas, and the pink barrette."

"'Tip number three'—guys, you're not listening!" Brenda burst out.

"Nancy," George said suddenly. "What if the thief is someone we haven't even thought about? Maybe what Brenda said yesterday was right. Maybe there's a crazy bike thief on the loose in River Heights!"

Brenda beamed. "I'm glad *someone* appreciates my brilliant ideas," she said.

Nancy frowned. "I guess it's possible," she said slowly. "But if the thief was just a crazy bike robber, why didn't he steal my bike and Bess's bike, too?"

No one had an answer to that.

* * * *

"There's been a rash of bike thefts in River Heights," Mr. Hamilton said.

It was Wednesday morning. Nancy, Bess, George, and Brenda were at Bike Mania with George's mother, Mrs. Fayne. Mrs. Fayne had wanted to talk to Mr. Hamilton about George's missing bike.

"A rash of bike thefts?" Mrs. Fayne repeated. "That's awful! How many bikes have been stolen that you know of?"

"Three in the last few weeks," Mr. Hamilton replied. "This is the first case of a child's bike being stolen, though. But rest assured, Mrs. Fayne. The police are working to find George's bike and the other bikes, too."

While Mrs. Fayne and Mr. Hamilton talked, Nancy started wandering around the store. Bess, George, and Brenda followed her.

"What are you looking for, Nancy?" Bess asked her.

"Clues," Nancy replied. "I still think it's weird that the bike thief didn't take my bike and Bess's bike too."

"Maybe he *was* going to take your bike and Bess's bike, but ran out of time," George suggested.

Nancy passed the section with all the brand-new kids' bikes. She ran her hand over their shiny metal handlebars. She wished *something* would come to her—some idea of how to find George's missing bike. The race was in only three more days. Time was running out!

As she walked, she came upon a familiar-looking blue door that said PRIVATE. It was open a crack.

That's the door that leads to the Re-Cycles workshop, Nancy thought. She wondered if Slam and Tia were working on old bikes in there. *It might be a good idea to talk to them about George's bike,* she thought. They might have some information. She poked her head through the crack.

"Stop!" someone cried from behind her. "You can't go in there!"

6

The White Bicycle

Y ou can't go in there!" the person repeated.

Nancy turned around. Tia was standing there.

Tia was wearing a pink T-shirt and jeans that were streaked with purple paint. She was holding a paintbrush in her right hand. She looked nervous.

"I'm sorry," Nancy apologized right away. "I wasn't going to go in there without permission. I just wanted to see if you and Slam were in there."

"We're working on some bikes for my dad," Tia mumbled. "We can't talk to you right now."

"I wanted to ask you if you knew anything about George's missing bike," Nancy went on. "You must notice a lot of bikes around the neighborhood. George's was kind of special."

"A white ABT Road Lizard," George piped up. "They don't make that model anymore."

Tia shook her head so hard that strands of her honey-blond hair tumbled out of her pink scrunchie. "No, uh-uh, I've never even heard of that kind of bike," she said. "I've got to go now. Bye!"

Tia quickly slipped past Nancy and her friends. She disappeared through the blue door marked PRIVATE and closed it. Nancy heard the *click* of a lock.

"Well, *she* wasn't very friendly," Brenda remarked.

"She seemed pretty friendly when we met her the other day," Bess said. "She must be having a bad day or something."

Nancy frowned. Why did Tia act like that? Was there something—or someone—behind the blue door that she didn't want Nancy and the others to see?

* * * *

"Pass the guacamole, please, Daddy," Nancy said.

"No problem, Pudding Pie," Carson Drew said cheerfully. He handed Nancy a white bowl filled with yummy homemade guacamole.

Mr. Drew had blue eyes that were just like Nancy's. He was a lawyer, so he was usually dressed in a business suit and tie. That night, however, he was dressed for a casual dinner at home: jeans and a button-down blue shirt.

Hannah was out with a friend. So Nancy and Mr. Drew had decided to have "Do It Yourself Taco Night" at home. There were plates of taco shells, grated cheese, refried beans, spicy and mild salsa, and other taco ingredients on the table.

"So how is your bicycle thief case coming along?" Mr. Drew asked Nancy as he heaped some spicy salsa on his taco.

Nancy told her father about their two suspects, Marianne and Lucas. She told him about the pink barrette that she had found in the muddy groove of George's bicycle tire. And she told him about the bike thief on the loose in River Heights.

"We have to catch George's bike thief soon," Nancy finished. "The bike race and rodeo are in three days!"

Mr. Drew nodded. "That's not very much time. Maybe George is going to have to borrow a bike for the race. Or maybe her parents are going to have to buy her a new bike."

"Her parents told her they would," Nancy said. "But she really, really wants to ride her white bike for the race. She said there's no way she can get used to a new bike by Saturday."

"Hmm," Mr. Drew said. "I guess you need to find her bike, then." He added, "So what's your next step?"

"I want to talk to our suspects again tomorrow," Nancy replied. "Tonight, I want to do some research about bicycle thieves on the Internet."

"Good idea," Mr. Drew said, nodding.

After dinner, Nancy helped her father wash the dishes. Then she went to the family computer and signed on to the Internet on her kids' account. She found a search program and typed in the words: *Bicycle thief, River Heights*.

A list of newspaper articles came up on the screen. Nancy clicked on the links and read the articles. They were all from the last few weeks.

The first article talked about a bike being stolen outside the Food Farm grocery store. The second one talked about a bike being stolen from somebody's driveway. The third article talked about a bike being stolen outside the high school.

Nancy noticed that the thief hadn't been caught yet. One of the articles said that the police had a description of the thief, though. According to the description, the thief was a man around twenty years old.

Nancy frowned. A man around twenty years old? That couldn't be George's bike thief, then. George's bike thief had been wearing a pink barrette!

Nancy continued looking around on the Internet. She read an article about ABT Road Lizards. She read an article about

Bike Mania, and one about the Re-Cycles program.

On the Re-Cycles home page was a picture of a poster Nancy had seen at Bike Mania. It had a picture of a blond girl with sunglasses standing next to a red bike and the words SPREAD THE JOY OF CYCLING BY RE-CYCLING!

Nancy stared at the picture. There was something about the picture that seemed important. *What is it?* she asked herself. But she couldn't pin it down.

"Come on, you slowpokes!" Brenda said. "We have detective work to do!"

Nancy, Bess, and George exchanged a glance. It was Thursday morning, and the four girls were on their way to talk to their two main suspects, Marianne and Lucas.

The girls had gotten permission from their parents to walk over to Marianne's and Lucas's houses. They were just arriving at Marianne's house.

"I have a new theory about this mystery," Brenda said, pausing at the end of Marianne's driveway. "I think it's an international bike

54

thief ring. They're going all over the world and stealing bikes."

"And they decided to come to River Heights?" George asked her with a frown.

Brenda nodded. "Yes! It's going to make a great story for my dad's paper. 'International Bike Thieves Target Paris, London, Tokyo, and River Heights!'"

"Hmm," Bess murmured doubtfully.

"Hey, there's Marianne," Nancy said, pointing.

Marianne was just pulling out of her driveway. She turned right and headed away from the four girls. She was riding a white bicycle.

It was George's bike!

7

Brenda to the Rescue

Marianne pedaled faster and cruised down the street.

"That's my bike!" George cried out. "Hey!"

Nancy and the three girls started running after Marianne. "Marianne! Stop! Marianne!" they all yelled.

Marianne glanced over her shoulder. When she realized that Nancy and her friends were chasing her, she braked to a stop.

The girls caught up to her. Marianne took off her bike helmet and giggled. "Hey! Why are you guys chasing me all the time? Hi, Brenda," she said, noticing Brenda for the first time.

"Hey, Marianne. Since our moms are friends, can I have an exclusive interview?" Brenda asked. She whipped out her notebook and pen. "Why did you do it, Marianne? Was it greed? Once you saw George's bike, you just couldn't help yourself, right?"

Marianne frowned. "Huh? What are you talking about, Brenda?"

George pointed to the bike. "You stole my bike—again!" she exclaimed. "Give it back, you thief!"

Marianne frowned. "*Your* bike? It's *my* bike," she said.

George's hands flew to her hips. "What are you talking about? It's *my* bike."

"This is great stuff for my article," Brenda said, scribbling like mad. "Keep arguing, guys!"

"I kept begging my parents for an ABT Road Lizard, so they finally bought me one," Marianne explained to George. "They gave it to me yesterday, as an early birthday present. The thing is, they could only find a pink one. So they had it painted white for me, as a surprise. They know I don't like pink. And they knew I wanted white."

"How can anyone not like pink?" Bess said, looking shocked.

Nancy bent down and studied Marianne's bike. She ran her fingers over the frame.

She picked at the underside of the frame with her fingernail. A tiny sliver of white paint came off. Underneath, she could see a speck of metallic pink.

"Marianne's telling the truth," Nancy told George. "This isn't your bike. It's a pink bike that was painted white."

"Oh," George said sheepishly. "I'm sorry, Marianne. I shouldn't have called you a thief!"

Marianne giggled again. "That's okay. I hope you find your bike soon. Then we can ride our white Road Lizards together!"

"Lucas lives in that house over there," George said. She pointed to a yellow house across the street and one over from her house.

The four girls looked both ways, then crossed the street. They walked up to the Wylies' front door and knocked.

"Let me do all the talking," Nancy whispered to her friends. "That means you, too, Brenda!"

"No problem," Brenda said cheerfully. "You're the boss!"

There was the loud sound of barking from inside the house. The door opened, and a tiny white poodle flung itself at the screen, barking and yipping.

Lucas appeared at the door. "Be quiet, Bruno! What do you guys want?" he snapped at Nancy and her friends.

Brenda stepped forward. She whipped out her notebook and pen.

"Lucas Wylie? Brenda Carlton," Brenda said crisply. "Do you want to make a comment for the newspaper about why you stole George Fayne's bike?"

"Brenda!" Nancy scolded.

Lucas made a face at Brenda. "Huh? What did you say?"

"I said, why did you steal George Fayne's bike?" Brenda repeated patiently.

Lucas glanced at George. "*Why* would I do a dumb thing like that?" he said.

"Because you'll do anything to win the bike race!" George blurted out.

"Besides, we heard you and your friend talking at the Double Dip," Brenda added. "Let's see, what were your exact words? You said, 'Now I'm definitely going to beat George Fayne!'"

"That means you stole her bike," Bess piped up. "You probably left the pink barrette there to confuse people and make them think it was a *girl* thief!"

Nancy frowned. Brenda, Bess, and George had totally taken over. Nancy hadn't even had a chance to talk.

Lucas was silent for a moment. He seemed to be thinking about something. Then he started cracking up.

"You guys are totally nuts!" he said finally. "I was telling my friend Stephan about my awesome new bike tires that I just bought. They have superfast treads, and they're going to help me win the race. *That's* what I was talking about."

Nancy and her friends stared at each other. "Oh," Nancy said after a moment.

"Oops! Sorry!" George apologized.

Lucas smiled meanly. "Don't worry about it, Fayne. Just start preparing yourself for total and absolute defeat on Saturday! And don't forget about my extra-large hot fudge sundae at the Double Dip."

Nancy sighed. Another dead end!

Nancy and her friends sat on the front steps of George's house. They tried to figure out what to do next.

"So Marianne and Lucas are probably innocent," Bess said. "Now what?"

"Maybe it's that professional bike thief, after all," George said. "You know, the one Mr. Hamilton was telling us about?"

"I don't know," Nancy said doubtfully. "I was reading about that thief on the Internet last night. It didn't sound like our thief."

"We just have to find whoever stole George's bike," Brenda said in a whiny voice. "Otherwise, my article will be totally boring!"

Nancy reached into her backpack and pulled out her blue detective notebook. She turned to the page that said "The Case of George's Missing Bike."

She ran her finger down the page. "There's one thing we should think about some more," she said. "The pink barrette clue."

Bess nodded. "Definitely. If we can figure out who owns the pink barrette, we can figure out who the thief is!"

Nancy closed her eyes and concentrated very hard. Where had she seen a pink barrette lately?

And then she remembered. She opened her eyes and smiled excitedly at her friends. "I think I've solved the mystery," she announced. "We have to get to my house right away!"

8

The Finish Line

What is this all about?" Hannah asked as Nancy and her friends burst through the front door.

"We're about to crack the case of George's bicycle thief!" Brenda said. "I *think*. Right, Nancy?"

"Right." Nancy led Hannah, Brenda, Bess, and George to the family computer.

"My stolen bike is in your house?" George asked, looking confused.

Nancy shook her head. "No, not exactly."

Nancy sat down at the computer. She turned it on and signed on to the Internet.

"What are you doing, Nancy?" Bess asked her, curious.

"Hang on," Nancy replied.

Nancy typed in some commands. After a moment, she reached the Re-Cycles Web site.

The picture of the blond girl with sunglasses came up on the screen. Nancy scrunched up close and studied the picture carefully.

"There!" Nancy exclaimed. She jabbed her finger at the screen. "This girl is wearing two pink barrettes!"

"Way to go, Nancy!" George cried out. Then she frowned. "But who *is* this girl?"

Nancy squinted at the screen. She couldn't tell who the girl was because she was wearing sunglasses.

"I wish I could make the picture bigger," Nancy said.

"I know how to do that!" Brenda offered.

"You do?" Bess asked her.

Brenda nodded. "I do it at my dad's office all the time."

"My goodness! You kids with your

high-tech computer skills," Hannah said, her eyes wide.

Nancy scooted over on her chair so Brenda could sit down next to her. Brenda started typing in different commands.

Within seconds the picture of the girl had zoomed to five times its size.

"Way to go, Brenda!" Nancy said excitedly.

Brenda grinned. "Thanks!"

Nancy studied the picture again. She pointed at the barrettes in the girl's hair. "They're definitely zigzaggy, like the one we found," she said.

Then Nancy noticed something. She pointed to a necklace that the girl was wearing. It looked like a silver necklace with letters on it.

"Can you make that bigger, Brenda?" Nancy said.

Brenda nodded. "Sure!"

Brenda typed in more commands. The necklace got bigger and bigger. The letters became larger too.

Nancy, George, Bess, Brenda, and Hannah all gasped at the same time.

The letters were TIA.

"Tia's the thief?" George said, amazed. "But why would she steal my bike? Her dad runs a bike store. She could have any bike she wants!"

"I don't know," Nancy said slowly. "*That's* still a mystery. We'd better go and talk to her right away."

Nancy, Hannah, and the three girls reached Bike Mania twenty minutes later in Hannah's car. Hannah told them she'd wait for them in the car. When the girls entered the store, Mr. Hamilton was standing behind the counter, talking to a customer.

"Hi, there," Mr. Hamilton said with a friendly wave. "What can I do for you today? George, have you found your bike yet?"

"Yes!" George said.

"No, not yet!" Nancy said at the same time.

Nancy gave George a warning look. She didn't want Mr. Hamilton to know that his daughter was a suspect.

"Are Slam and Tia around?" Nancy asked Mr. Hamilton.

"They're in the Re-Cycles room, working on some bikes," he replied. "Go on back there. I'm sure they'll be glad to see you."

Or maybe not, Nancy thought. She thanked Mr. Hamilton and headed toward the back of the store. The three girls followed.

The blue door marked PRIVATE was closed. Nancy put her ear up to the door.

She could hear Tia and Slam's voices coming from the other side. They seemed to be arguing about something.

Nancy knocked on the door. The arguing stopped suddenly.

Without waiting for an invitation, Nancy opened the door. "Hello?" she called out.

Slam was sitting cross-legged on the floor, fixing a flat tire. Tia was polishing up a kid's purple bike. As soon as she saw Nancy, she scrambled to her feet. She looked upset.

"I hope I'm not bothering you guys," Nancy said.

"Well, actually, we're superbusy," Tia said nervously.

Tia glanced over her shoulder, then

moved a few inches to the right. Nancy wondered what she was doing.

Then she realized that Tia was standing in front of the purple bike she had been working on. In fact, Tia seemed to be trying to hide the bike.

Why would she do that? Nancy wondered. Then it came to her.

Marianne's parents had given her a pink ABT Road Lizard that had been painted white.

Yesterday Nancy had noticed Tia with purple paint all over her clothes.

Tia was working on a purple bike now—a bike she seemed to want to hide from Nancy and her friends.

"Tia," Nancy said slowly. "Is that George's ABT Road Lizard? Did you paint it purple?"

Tia's face turned bright red. She stared at her feet.

"Um, kind of," Tia whispered.

"Th-that's my b-bike?" George burst out. "What did you do to it? Why is it all purple like that?"

Slam stood up and put his hand on his

sister's shoulder. "Tell them, Tia," he urged her.

Tia glanced up. Her eyes were shiny with tears. "I'm really, really sorry," she said to George. "It was a big mistake! See, on Tuesday someone was supposed to drop off a white ABT Road Lizard to donate to the Re-Cycles program. Dad told me that when it showed up, it was my job to clean it up and paint it purple. There's a girl on the Re-Cycles wish list who really, really wants a purple mountain bike."

"But I didn't donate my bike to the Re-Cycles program!" George pointed out.

"I know," Tia said. "That's where the mistake part comes in. It turns out that the guy who was going to donate his white Road Lizard changed his mind. But I didn't know that. When I saw your bike lying in the grass, George, I thought that was *his* bike. I took it into the store and started cleaning it up and painting it right away."

"That's why we saw purple paint on your clothes yesterday," Nancy said.

Tia nodded. "Slam is the one who figured out the mix-up," she went on. "He told me I should tell Dad right away. But I was way too embarrassed to tell Dad what I'd done. I thought he might get really mad at me. I'm really sorry!" She stared at George, her lip quivering.

George shrugged. "It's okay. I guess mistakes happen."

"I'll repaint it white for you, if you want," Tia offered.

"Maybe after the race on Saturday, okay? I want to take my bike home right away and start practicing," George replied.

"Come on, let's go tell Dad everything," Slam said, taking Tia by the arm.

Tia nodded. "I guess I'd better."

"Mystery solved," Nancy said, relieved.

George reached over and gave Nancy a big hug. "Thank you for finding my bike!" she said happily.

Brenda whipped out her reporter's notebook. "This is going to be the most awesome newspaper story!" she exclaimed.

The day of the race was a beautiful sunny day. There was a huge crowd in the parking lot of Bike Mania. People were cheering and waving banners that said things like GOOD LUCK, JESSICA! and NEVON IS #1! Hannah and Mr. Drew were holding up a banner that said WAY TO GO, NANCY! The Faynes and Marvins had similar banners for George and Bess, too.

Nancy, George, and Bess were waiting at the starting line along with a bunch of other kids their age. There were ten kids in all, including Lucas Wylie. All of them were wearing bike helmets. The races for older kids would happen later.

Nancy gave George a thumbs-up. George was on her bike, which was still purple. "Good luck!" Nancy called out.

"Good luck!" George called back.

Mr. Hamilton blew the starter whistle. Nancy and the rest of the contestants took off. The crowd yelled with excitement.

The neighborhood had been blocked off from cars so the bike race could take place. Nancy kept her eye on the road and pedaled like mad. She was pedaling so fast that her legs got tired pretty quickly. But she kept going.

All of a sudden she felt someone pass her

on the left. It was George! A second later someone passed her on the right. It was Lucas!

The contestants rounded the final corner and hurried down the final stretch toward the finish line. George and Lucas were neck and neck. Nancy was in third place. Bess was somewhere behind her.

Nancy put on a final burst of speed. Her legs ached, but she pumped hard anyway.

Right before the finish line, she passed Lucas. But George pulled ahead. George came in first!

The crowd roared with applause. "Yay, George!" Mr. and Mrs. Fayne cried out. "Way to go!"

Nancy came in second. Lucas came in third. Nancy got off her bike and rushed up to George. They exchanged a big hug.

"Congratulations!" Nancy said to George.

"Congratulations!" George said to Nancy.

Lucas came up to both of them. "Uh, congratulations, I guess," he mumbled.

George grinned. "I guess someone owes me a sundae at the Double Dip!" she teased.

"Yeah." Lucas pouted.

"Still, you came in third. That's awesome. Congratulations, Lucas!" George said.

Brenda hurried up to the winners. She had her notebook in hand. "Does anyone want to make a comment for the newspaper? How does it feel to win, George? Did you cheat or anything like that?" Brenda said breathlessly.

George giggled. Nancy giggled too. Brenda was back to her old self!

That night, before going to bed, Nancy pulled out her notebook and wrote:

Today was superexciting. George won the bike race, and I came in second. Bess came in first in the obstacle course. It was a big day for all of us!

George got the grand prize, a white mountain bike. She decided to give her old bike to the girl who really wanted the purple Road Lizard. The girl was at the race, and she was really happy.

The police caught the real thief who's been stealing all the bikes around River Heights. He was a man from Chicago

and all the bikes were returned to their owners. I'm glad that mystery was solved too!

But the best part about this case was Brenda. She really helped us out this time!

It just goes to show that just as bikes can have more than one layer of paint, people have layers too. Brenda is not so bad after all. I'm sure glad she helped us solve this mystery on wheels!

CASE CLOSED!